D0535705

YUBA COUNTY LIBRARY
MARYSVILLE, CA

First published in Great Britain in 2003 by Brimax™,
an imprint of Octopus Publishing Group Ltd
2-4 Heron Quays, London E14 4JP

Text and illustrations copyright © Octopus Publishing Ltd 2003

Mc Graw Hill **Children's Publishing**

All rights reserved. Except as permitted under the United States Copyright Act, no part of this publication may be reproduced or distributed in any form or by any means, or stored in a database retrieval system, without prior written permission from the publisher.

This edition published in the United States of America in 2003 by
Gingham Dog Press
an imprint of McGraw-Hill Children's Publishing,
a Division of The McGraw-Hill Companies
8787 Orion Place
Columbus, Ohio 43240-4027

www.MHkids.com

Library of Congress Cataloging-in-Publication Data is on file with the publisher.

Printed in China.

1-57768-480-X (HC)   1-57768-927-5 (PB)

1 2 3 4 5 6 7 8 9 10 BRI 09 08 07 06 05 04 03

Ping Won't Share!

By
Lynne Gibbs

GINGHAM DOG
PRESS

Columbus, Ohio

Illustrated by
Melanie Mitchell

Ping and his friends, Shi Shi and Yang, were very hungry. Their favorite food was bamboo, but they were running out of the leafy branches. With their tummies rumbling, they searched the whole forest, but they couldn't find any more bamboo.

"What will we do if we can't find any food?" cried Shi Shi.

"Let's look one more time," said Yang. "We'll go in separate directions and meet back here later."

Ping trudged through the forest searching for food. He crawled through an area he'd never been to before. Right in front of him stood a large patch of bamboo! Ping could not believe his good luck!

Sitting under a tree, Ping munched his way through a leafy pile of bamboo. Then he rubbed his full tummy and sighed happily.

This will last me for days, thought Ping. But I won't tell anyone else what I've found. Otherwise, they might want some too.

Later, just as the sun was going down, Ping and his friends sat in a circle and shared their last branch of bamboo. Ping took just a small bite and left the rest for the others.

"How do you stay so big and strong when you eat so little, Ping?" asked Yang.

"Oh, I don't need much food," replied Ping, thinking of his secret supper. He was beginning to feel guilty.

When his friends slept that night, Ping lay wide awake.

I'm being greedy keeping all that bamboo to myself, he thought.

But the next morning, when Ping's tummy rumbled, he quickly changed his mind. Sneaking away, Ping crept to the pile of bamboo he had found and had a breakfast feast all by himself.

When Ping got back, a nosy pheasant spoke to them all. "I know where you can find bamboo," he squawked from his perch on a branch. He pointed his wing toward a snow-covered peak in the distance. "It grows on that mountainside."

With that, Ping's friends decided it was time to leave their homes and travel far away in search of food.

When Ping told his friends that he was not leaving with them, they looked very sad.

"I'm happy here and I don't need much food to keep me fit and strong," lied Ping.

Waving goodbye, Yang and Shi Shi set off on their long journey.

"I hope you find lots of bamboo," called Ping. As he watched them leave, Ping wished he could have given his friends just a little bamboo for their trip. But if I had, they would have asked where it came from, he thought with a sigh. And I wouldn't want to share it all.

At first, Ping was quite happy. He had the birds and the butterflies to keep him company, and there was plenty to eat. But as the days passed, Ping grew very lonely and missed his friends. Plus, his supply of bamboo grew smaller and smaller until one day there was nothing left. Ping rubbed his rumbling tummy and thought about his friends in their new home.

One afternoon, as Ping searched for tiny scraps of bamboo, the pheasant swooped down.

"It's too bad you didn't go with your friends," chirped the bird. "They found lots of bamboo and cozy new homes."

"If only I had shared my bamboo," said a lonely and hungry Ping. "I wouldn't be all alone with nothing to eat."

Settling back down in his favorite spot, Ping remembered how much fun he used to have playing with Shi Shi and Yang. He missed their games of hide-and-seek.

Big tears began to roll down his face as he remembered how badly he had treated his friends. He was soon sobbing so loudly that he almost didn't hear two familiar voices calling out, "Hello, Ping!"

"Don't cry, Ping," said Shi Shi and Yang as they gathered around him. "We've come back to share the bamboo we found."

Wiping away his tears, Ping jumped to his feet and hugged his friends.

"I've missed you two so much!" he cried. Ping felt very ashamed of his selfishness and told his friends all about the supply of bamboo he'd kept for himself.

Yang and Shi Shi stared angrily at Ping. "How could you just let us go hungry?" demanded Yang.

"You've been very selfish," said Shi Shi, shaking her head.

"I'm so sorry," said Ping. "Will you please forgive me?" He felt very sad.

When Ping said he had learned his lesson, his friends forgave him. They shared some of their bamboo with Ping since they knew he would need strength for the journey ahead.

"From now on, we'll always stick together," said Shi Shi.

"From now on, I'll always share with my friends," promised Ping. Munching their bamboo happily, the three pandas watched the sun set over their new home.

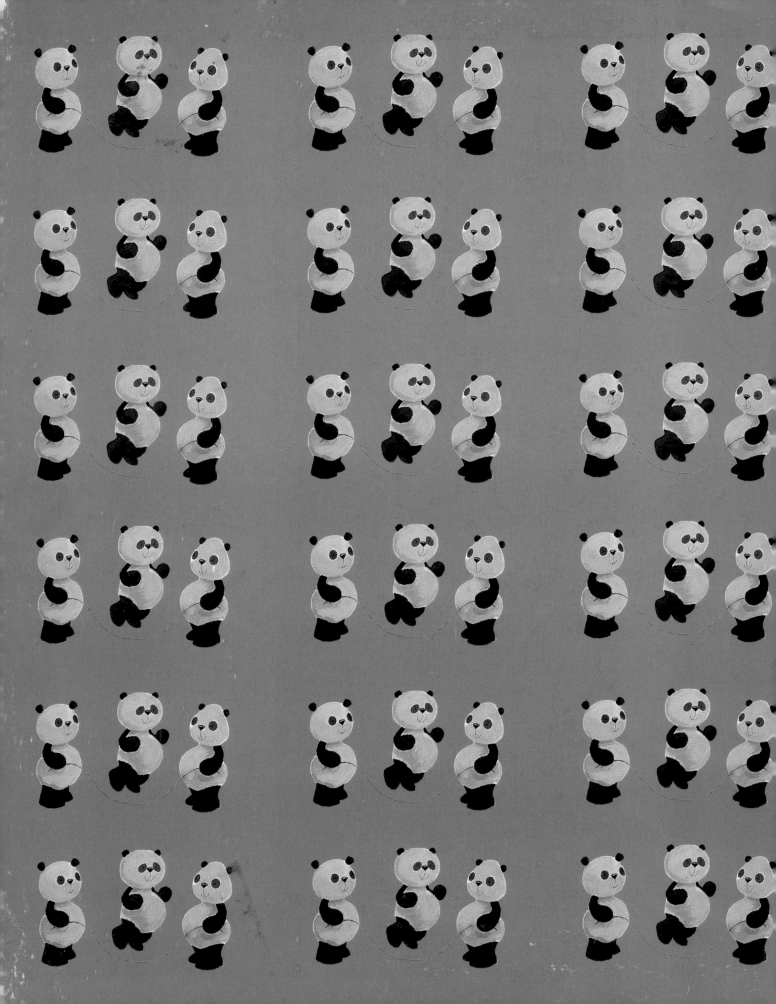